Bob's Egg Hunt

A Lift-the-Flap Story

by Annie Auerbach

illustrated by
Barry Goldberg

SIMON SPOTLIGHT
An imprint of Simon & Schuster Children's Publishing Division
New York   London   Toronto   Sydney   Singapore
1230 Avenue of the Americas, New York, New York 10020

Manufactured in China   ISBN 0-689-84590-1   First Edition
2 4 6 8 10 9 7 5 3 1

One spring day Bob and his team were hard at work helping Farmer Pickles in the fields. Lofty and Muck were clearing out some branches, while Dizzy and Roley were fixing a road.

"Scoop, I need you to dig holes for a new fence," Bob said.

"No prob, Bob!" Scoop replied.

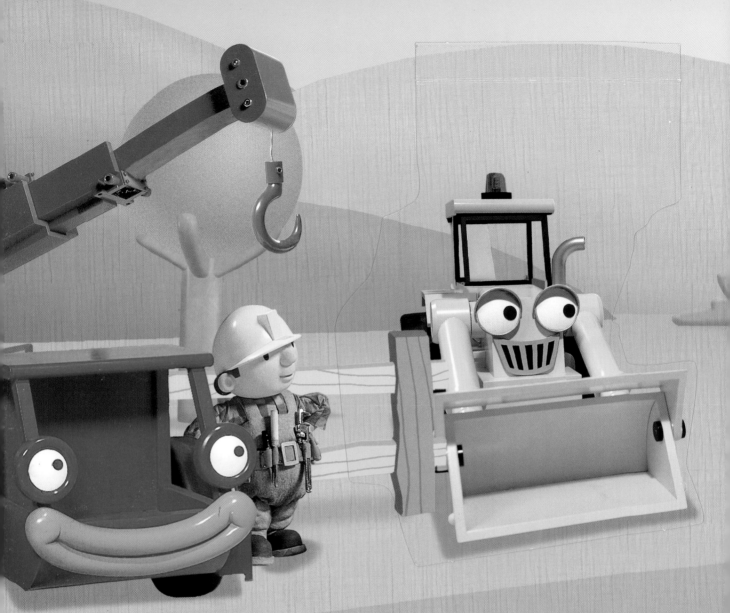

Soon it was time to take a break.

"What a beautiful spring day it is!" Scoop exclaimed.

"It sure is! And in honor of spring, I have a surprise for all of you.
We're going to play a game of hide-and-seek!" Bob said.

"Yippee!" squealed Dizzy. "I *love* that game! What are we looking for?"
"I've hidden some colorful eggs on the farm," Bob explained, "for all of you to find!"

The machines split up, and the egg hunt was on!

"Let's look over here," suggested Roley. He wanted to be the first to find an egg.

"Be careful! Don't roll over the flowers," Scoop warned.
The team found lots of things, but no eggs.

Lofty used his hook to search for eggs in a tree.

Muck searched for eggs under some hay bales.

Dizzy thought she found some eggs in a tree.

"Yippee!" she cried. Dizzy *had* found an egg . . . but it belonged to someone else!

Everyone gathered back at the farm.
"So, how many eggs did you find?" Bob asked the team.
"None," they all replied sadly.

Bob scratched his head. Then he asked the machines where they had looked, and he discovered that no one had checked the barn.

"What if Travis picked them up?" Lofty asked.

"Or Farmer Pickles?" suggested Roley.

At the barn poor Spud was holding his stomach.
"What's wrong, Spud?" Bob asked.
"Oh, I ate too many chocolate eggs!" he moaned.
"So *that's* where they went!" laughed Bob.